BEHIND

the

WALL

By Dame DJ
©Dame DJ 2015

Sign up to see new releases, Audio books mailing list &
get a

FREE eBook

Join us @

www.DJBooks.Club

Individual support & confidential discussions can be
arranged details on

www.DJBooks.Club

7 days advance booking needed on GMT

request dates via;

damedj@djbooks.club

PART 1

Miami here I come.

Dragging suitcases from baggage reclaim in the heat of Miami airport was always a potential heart attack, and I scanned the lounge amazed that no one was physically slumped over their trolley, overcome with stress. One of the baggage handlers might have tossed them down some revolving if they looked that vulnerable.

The freezing air-conditioning never helped the intense atmosphere as this was the gateway to South America, with bad tempered immigration officials who started through glassy cold eyes treating us like felons, regardless of which flight we came in on.

I ignored the customs agents and lumbered with determination towards the exit door hauling over-packed, bulging suitcases.

Heading out towards the beeping, chaotic traffic the electric doors opened, throwing me against a wall of buzzing heat, and the first breaths of humid, still, thick air filled my lungs like syrup.

This was Jurassic, like the beginning of time; when the earth was bubbling hot, insect-ridden and dangerous.

Suntanned Spanish drivers hooted and braked like emergencies and fought for position as if arriving with dying patients. I lumbered past them also.

Whisked away in a white limo I fell back into a world of still motionless cold air, tinted windows, gentle noises and relative safety.

He hit the pedal, I hit the vodka, and we headed top speed up the I-95.

The Interstate 95 gleamed like the *yellow brick road*, generously accommodating thousands of screeching cars and trucks rushing north and south like escaping insects.

The race was on…'hello Florida'.

❊   ❊   ❊

Early the next morning, the sun rose to a perfectly clear blue sky and I jumped out of bed, grabbed the car keys and set out for supplies.

I bought a ludicrously small amount of food and some fresh rolls to ensure I would *have* to return the next day and every day from then on.

Florida was bathed in a late November golden morning glow; the air was crisp and a few little puffs of white clouds drifted overhead like small children going to school.

This was the beginning of their winter season with crisp morning, a few showers, blue skies and gentle breezes; a climate the rest of us only dream about.

Water sprinklers angled in all directions, dribbled and spat watering the pathways like mini waterfalls in an aqua shows without the dancers. Dewdrops clung to the Colombian emerald grass; shimmering in the sunlight it looked succulent, nourishing yet untouchable.

Pulling into the empty parking lot, I headed for a large primrose-yellow supermarket with eyelash awnings in striped black, white, and yellow. Young palm trees stood in line waiting endlessly, slim, proud, with green feathery tops and not a hair out of place.

I pulled in wide, with the choice of any parking place I wanted. Overhead the sound of melodious music and native birds competed with each other, or perhaps the birds all knew the chorus to the songs that were playing?

Electric doors parted and a blast of freezing air slapped me hard in the face, like an invisible iceberg.

Abundant pyramids of fruit and vegetables lay before me in perfect array brightly polished, the same size and all facing forward.

Every one was a jewel, a fine specimen, a perfect replica of each other, and too beautiful to touch. They looked like family.

Avocados, red peppers, oranges, bananas, and lemons; a rainbow of colors with not a hint of soil, dirt or farmers hands on them to be seen.

I stopped, stared, appreciated and admired but I passed on as I today only needed two bread rolls for breakfast but I would be back tomorrow at same time.

This was heaven, but I couldn't stay too long.

Welcome to Florida.

* * *

Unpacking in someone else's house was exciting, especially one as pretty and well taken care of as this which Tim had rented for us from the November to April winter season.

Driving through the security gate of the golf development, another smart security guard carefully inspected our details, made a call, and lifted the barrier.

Heavy with gold brocade and black cap, he looked like he had fought in the last war, but had missed out on the medals and was now in command of a golfing community.

At the junction was the biggest Banyan tree I had ever seen which became an important landmark; we turned left, continued past several identical turnings that felt surreal like a Levittown development.

They had the same gardens, same driveways, same post boxes and front doors but with different small black numbers.

We were at 125th Avenue, two houses in from the right like a huge parking lot just full of the same houses. It looked like Lego land made of geometric shapes, angular roofs, some round windows, and equal driveways.

The gardens were all landscaped exactly the same way but with a few very subtle variations of about six different plants so they matched up like uniforms.

I looked for open garden gates, children climbing over and under; young mothers chatting to neighbors, baking fresh cookies, and everyone being part of a close community. I saw none.

Cream garbage bins stood like pillars to the left and right on the drive, and a little paved path ran down the side of the house for pool access, but there was no individuality.

I was going to have to learn that *was* the point - smart, simple, and designed living not cluttered by lots of messy 'individuals'.

There were going to be signs of life, but this was a Florida Gated Golf Community, behind a wall, and they were not going to be what I had imagined.

❖   ❖   ❖

Moving into our cappuccino-cream contemporary new house with white floor so clean you could role pastry out on them, was exciting, fresh, and sheer pleasure.

We had a white corner bath, with a Jacuzzi, double sinks, and a huge walk-in shower all lit up from a skylight above so we could see a galaxy of stars at night. Tall mirrors on each wall reflected us naked, and into infinity.

The bedroom had two walk-in closets, one on each side, and a piece of large decorative furniture for a huge TV and two bedside tables with elegant lamps.

Most importantly, we had French doors leading straight to a screened in pool! How romantic, how sensational, how thoughtful of the builder! He could have simply put in windows and saved the money.

The outdoor screens puzzled me at first as they dimmed the view, and I didn't see any bugs so immediately opened them and the windows up, but Tim quickly slammed them shut and mumbled about air conditioning.

No matter, I was still happy, so I ignored it all and never thought to wonder just how cold-blooded Tim really was.

The small pool wasn't heated but I imagined lovely evenings, Martinis, music, and midnight swims.

For a girl born in the tropics, taken to England to shiver and freeze, I was now close to blue skies, yellow sun, and fresh air, but the doors and windows had to remain firmly shut so we could live in a fridge.

This was a Florida Golf & Country Club community and I was naïve - happy, but naïve.

        ❋   ❋   ❋

Passing the magnificent clock tower at the gate on the way out I didn't bother to check the time as it was like being in Disney World, and time would not have mattered.

The immaculate security men, clothed in brocade and military style coats waved us on as we left; they were not in the business of keeping people in.

The automatic barrier lifted and we drove passed rich green hedges, fountains, and flowerbeds, and headed for the outside world.

It felt like time passed by differently out here, and we only went out for necessities like petrol, food, newspapers, haircuts, and anything else that didn't revolve around country club living.

You could lose a couple of days, miss world events, forget the date, and only watch the selected American news they chose to air including snippets of useless adverts or information mixed with an unusual amount of local violence.

There were no seasonal changes here, just slight temperature changes that could throw a day's activity into turmoil.

People originally from huge distances away that had been used to extreme conditions in the Northern USA or Canada, were now suddenly very indignant that a golf tee-off time might be postponed if some rumbling nebulous grey clouds gathered on the horizon.

Bad weather put fear into men's hearts, and frizz into women's hair. The car parks emptied like War of the Worlds, and golf carts were abandoned on grass verges.

In the odd storm palm trees panicked and swayed, thrashing their green limbs about. Rains fell like a tantrum and manicured shrubs begrudgingly gave up a few odd leaves to the wind.

This picture perfect golfing community was not succumbing to climate change, as in a few hours, everything went back to normal like nothing had happened.

The weather was pure emotion; unpredictable, intense, then exhausted, submissive, and tranquil.

No wonder ancient man worshipped the sun.

Rules of the Game

It was time for another glass of freshly squeezed Florida orange juice that I had discovered like manna from heaven, and I headed for a pink tubular empty table.

"Morning"
"Hi there"
"Hello"
"All right today?"
 "When is your game?"
…Rang out all the greetings, and I was grateful to everyone for being so friendly.

I sat down and scanned the terrace for a waiter, while nodding at anyone who looked my way, regardless if we had ever been introduced.

My isolation was short-lived, as this was club life and everyone clustered into groups as quickly as possible as if they couldn't breathe alone.

For them making the right alliances from the beginning was crucial, as slipping down the social ladder was a constant fear, and moving back up was near impossible. I was an outsider and I didn't take it seriously.

Mistakenly, I had thought that allegiances were made between people that liked, respected, and were fond of each other, but it was more about being financially compatible.

Rich people rarely mixed or socialized with poor people, unless they were something interesting like artists - that had been exhibited of course.

The quickest of interviews were being given all around the club, and dismissal depended on your first reply.

Exchanging names was not an immediate formality, as that could wait until you had made up your mind, if or not you wanted to continue the conversation.

It was like 'speed dating' but in couples, and at a golf club.

"By the way, my name is John, and this is my wife Joan" was a typical introduction that could follow 45 minutes *after* quite a lot of detailed discussion on a huge range of topics.

Thinking people were friendly and open was partially true, but it was the quickest way of trying to place you socially and economically, and in order to do so, a lot of silly questions needed to be answered first.

"Are you living here?"
"Are you visiting and for how long?"
"Are you a golf or tennis member?"
"Where are your other homes?"
"Were do you eat?
"Who do you know?"
"What broker do you use?"
…And so on.

The wrong answer to one or more questions and the conversation was terminated, like a game of multiple choice, while scoring points put you into various categories.

It was something Tony Blair did not even remotely grasp when he was with George Bush, the sad fool thought we all spoke a common language. We do not-the words are the same but the meanings are different.

Jumping from a low score up to a higher score was possible if you had an overwhelming advantage like being famous, foreign, stunning, or a mafia family member.

Living in the right village was the 'color of your passport', because they assumed every human being on earth would buy the best possible house they could afford.

❊   ❊   ❊

Where to have dinner was the most important decision of the day, and it normally took all day to decide.

"We went to Renato's last night," called one person to another in the middle of playing tennis.

"Ball please! Oh, really…how was that? I heard they make good pasta."

"It was the best! I had the stuffed shells with ricotta," came a reply during a serve.

"OUT! That ball was out! Did you *see* that out?" came an irritated voice from the opposite side of the court, insisting in an authoritative tone.

Silence returned as they continued play back into the rhythm of the game, consumed by thoughts of shells and ricotta.

Having started at 8am, with nothing to eat or drink but a small juice, most of us were starving hungry.

The south of France had the aroma of lavender and perfumes, but Boca smelt of chips, BBQ ribs, muffins, and coffee, depending on what the hotel chefs were preparing.

The only way to avoid thinking about food was to think of something even more over whelming – sex, but as most people in country clubs were ageing, over medicated, and heavy, this was not a great solution.

I noticed during tennis the minute the opposition team were behind, they would shout "the veal chop was this thick and it cut like butter!" showing fingers to show just how thick.

Chasing a small lime green ball, in the heat, hungry and for no obvious reason, was something I had to learn to enjoy.

This was Florida and it would be a long winter so learning and observing their rules was going to be important.

Nibbles with Kitty and Scott

The members' committee spent all their waking hours dreaming up activities to keep hundreds of people of all ages and abilities amused.

Another body of people had ordered half a rain forest of paper to print up activity sheets and brochures to get the sleepiest members to sit up, join in, and take note.

Brochures filled with photos of palm trees, couples holding hands on golf courses, tennis courts with happy children and the obligatory golden sunsets.

They must have been snapped by paparazzi, hiding in bushes and waiting for those tender moments; none of which I ever saw in real life, except for the sunsets.

The monthly newssheet showed photos of sunburnt faces and revelers at the last Latin, Samba, or Calypso evening, all taken after cocktail hour.

These photos enforced a feeling of envy in anyone who missed the event, forgot to buy the ticket, or left early, as the events were so well promoted to have not gone would have been a sin.

The Friday night Happy Hour, from 5.30 to 8pm at the main clubhouse, was the very high point of the week.

Arriving was like gatecrashing a party; you had no idea who was the host or hostess, as no one gave any introductions, and it was each to his own.

It was up to us to approach strangers, introduce ourselves, find common interests, and end up being the best of friends.

I was good at this; I worked the room as if it was my own party, and ended up introducing couples to other couples. It gave me a freedom, and I needed it.

Everyone looked clean and smart at last compared to his or her previous wet and sweaty exercise clothes.

Wearing shoes, covering up bandy legs, hiding sagging bottoms was all a visual relief long over due we all owed each other.

Wear large gold earrings, lots of bracelets, a huge diamond ring, the longest glossy set of fingernails topped hands with delicately held chilled white wine glasses, the ladies smiled and chatted amicably.

The handbags were studded with enough metal to look like weapons; oversized belt buckles with animal heads squashed in thick waists topped by bouffant hair that never moved out of place.

None of the women were flat chested as they were either fat all over, or very thin with protruding, exposed silicone breasts demanding attention in their own right.

A few stragglers had lost the slimming war to anorexia or bulimia; with emaciated bodies serious enough to warrant a Red Cross visit to save the poor souls.

I wondered if some men had a silent terror of large breasts, and were actively searching for small ones.

Sporting bright reds, greens, yellows, and the crispest of whites, they paraded about like exotic parrots in warring colors that signaled a possible nasty peck.

The men looked like a pretty clean, neat, and well manicured lot, even if Mother Nature had not given them the best of looks.

A few showed a fabulous sense of humor by wearing 'rugs' plumped on their heads, like nesting sites for a passing sparrow.

The classic 'golf shirt' had saved many hours of wardrobe decisions, and they wore them in every shade of every color imaginable.

We walked over to the bar, already two rows deep, and four hundred pairs of predator eyes followed us on swiveling necks to take in all our details.

"Hello. How do you do?" I said to the woman on my right, as I outstretched my hand towards her. She was young with short brown hair and deep brown eyes.

She looked at my open hand, then back at me, and stared in shock.

"Oh, hi there. How are ya?" She replied.
"Fine, jolly good. It's so busy here - I didn't expect such a crowd." I smiled, and as she picked up my English accent, all the irritation of being interrupted immediately left her.

"This is my husband, Scott," she said, and she leaned back in her chair so I could get a better look at him.

"She's from England," she said to her husband, patting his arm like a secret sign that I was okay.

"Oh! *Top of the morning to you*! I was in London in 1989. Great city. Great. Love the people too. I was staying in Kensington, do you know it?" He asked.

I smiled, as no one had ever said 'top of the morning' to me, and probably never would.

He wanted to relive his trip and I was happy to hear about it. So much had changed in that great city, but they think it's all frozen in time.

I suppose in all of London's deep history, the passing of a few years later was nothing much to remark about.

Her husband had a huge body, with very wide shoulders that were used to pumping iron and topped with smallish head and boyish face. His beady, pale blue eyes focused on me eagerly starring out from a grey-colored damp face and he broke into a smile easily.

"You would love London honey," he kept saying to her as he recounted his happy days, during which I suspected there must have a couple of English girls who showed him the hotspots.
Business alone could never have been so much fun.

"I'll take you one day, I promise," he said and she patiently listened, nodding in agreement which indicated to me that must have been newlyweds, as her attention span had not yet gone.

"These are friends of ours; Eric is a scratch golfer, and this is his wife, Penny."

And so it went on with lively animated conversation. The drinks came and went, as did the piles of greasy morsels, and we felt we belonged somehow.

The room filled to capacity, and voices rose higher and higher, competing with each other in octaves like excited birds at feeding time.
8pm came quickly, and we had a dinner reservation nearby so we started to say our goodbyes.

As I stood up to go, I suddenly realized whom the girl Penny was.

Last week at the ladies' tennis clinic, I had noticed a short, petite blonde, whom I took to be about 24 years old, with tight Goldilocks hair and a slightly grey face. I took her under my wing, as I felt less conspicuous being protective of someone else.

"I remember you. You look so different out of tennis clothes!" I exclaimed.
"So do you," she replied through a smile, and I wondered what she meant.

"See you next Monday on the court!"
On the way out we said goodbye, kissed people we had never met, and waved at strangers; it felt like the natural thing to do. What a few cases of chardonnay can do for a crowd!

That was Friday nights taken care of for the season, and regular morning tennis game for me set on Monday's, which satisfied Tim's constant questions about possible games. I could not even play tennis but he chose to ignore that.

Things were looking up, we were settling in, making friends, finding our way but the patio doors remained tightly shut.

Iced water for Lee

"How are you doing today?" asked a middle aged, bronzed, male tennis player.

We were all sitting on a terrace by the courts; I had got the table first and was waiting for Tim to finish his game.

"Very well, thank you," I said in a matter-of-fact English accent, hoping he would leave quickly.

"That's real great. I'm Lee, in case you didn't know," he said, already moving off with his eyes on the courts ahead.
"No, I didn't know. But I certainly do now," I smiled to myself, knowing the accent can repel as well as attract depending on the pitch.

Bloody Limey he probably thought.

I had seen Lee many times at the gym; he looked like he had rebuilt his body through sheer perseverance.

If he had noticed me, it had not been by looking in my direction, so I assumed he hadn't seen me before today.

He played tennis with the same dedication as he pumped iron, and was good at both. His steel-framed glasses enlarged his fading watery blue-grey eyes, and they gave no hint of warmth. His perfect teeth were a fairly new physical addition, and he exposed them often in a kind of ritual smile to get his money's worth.

Next to the terrace was the tennis shop and booking office where all the courts were reserved and allocated.
On a slightly risen podium behind a long desk, the two blondes who ran the 28 courts competed with each other for dominance.

It was a daily beauty contest, and for most of the other women, it was quite inhibiting.

Their long fine tresses twirled into ponytails; sun visors and caps always looking immaculate, with tennis skirts, frilly white socks and tennis shoes they looked like overgrown sexy schoolgirls.

They had the power of the pencil, topped with rubbers that could 'rub' you off a court if you didn't pay sufficient respect and homage.

Everyone did, all of the time…or you never got to play.

The average middle-aged balding male player crawled in with his tongue hanging out, flirting desperately and trying to make an impression, but seldom achieved anything.

The women were either too menopausal, slightly pitiful, aggressive, or asked too many questions that needed too many replies, asked all their friends and then changed their minds.

I found my own balance with no help from the blondes. By being friendly, courteous, and genuine ensured me a warm welcome and considerate service.

"Court number 8, and you are the first! Have a great game!" She called over to me.
"Thank you," I waved, feeling good in yet another new outfit. I couldn't play very well, but I sure made an effort to look like I could.

Humiliation on court 8 was soon to come and bent down to pick up a million small lime green tennis balls and swore at every one of them.

I had to find someone who played as badly as I did and simply didn't care what a liability I really was.

A nice plump older lady came wandering over.

"Hello, I'm your partner this morning," she said.
God help you, I thought." I hope you like the English."

Villages

Coconut Boulevard, Palm Tree Drive, Willow's Creek...were whimsical names of the individual villages in the enormous golfing complex, all built around the central golf course.

A most wonderful concept! It didn't exactly replace the ancient village green, but given most English people could no longer afford a house overlooking a village green, this was an excellent idea and gave so many homes wonderful views.

The internal road was wide with undulating, smooth, rippling bends, edged with external green grasses that never died, alongside footpaths for the odd jogger.

These paths were never cluttered with pedestrians and never grew weeds or had litter. They were serene, empty, calm, and decorative. Why couldn't the whole world be like this?

Between the gym and the jogging, people burnt off enough spare and unwanted calories to feed a small African country.

Squirrels darted and ran for no good reason as there were no predators here and they were in no danger. Had they not been in the overall master plan they would have all been exterminated immediately, but they could stay if they didn't bury nuts on the golf course.

I lost my way as each perfect boulevard ran into the next and all the palm trees swayed in the same direction.

Clusters of houses in individually architecturally- designed villages branched off to the left or right in intervals of about half a mile.

Whispering Brook, Green Reeds, Barbados Sun, or Vintage Court all had a different price bracket, size of house, style, and location to the clubhouse. The names themselves made no sense at first, but when they came to represent a cluster of $2-3 million golf-view Spanish-style villas, it was surprising how quickly a name could become significant.

All the villages basically competed with each other with different grand entrances, gold lettering, fountains, marble entrances, and Italian-style ponds, but the price of the houses inside was set.

Majestic palm trees, arrays of endless flowers, lakes that never dried up, and tall grasses were only disturbed by the occasional visiting egret.

Underground pipes apparently connected the lakes, but I never saw a huge dinosaur of a gator basking motionless on a golf course as golf carts whisked around. I wondered how the club would have dealt with that.

Every day that passed, this place became more real.
We were here and you could touch, feel, and smell the nature around you, but it was the outer world on television and people in far off places, bombing, starving, fighting, and burning that become the more unreal.

Florida and our life behind the wall which was actually beginning to keep us in…voluntarily, of course for now.

❊   ❊   ❊

Back in the supermarket, Frank Sinatra and I waltzed between the pregnant chocolate muffins, trotted passed the sea green pickles, and swayed in front of exotic fruits and on towards the checkout girl, carrying, as usual, very little to eat.

They always avoided looking at my face, and only ever said "have a nice day," which they could very well have not meant, but I didn't care.

I was in heaven, happy to be alive; the world had no starvation as we lived in abundance and this was becoming my reality.

All human misery was a thing of the past. Man could organize himself if he had the will, money, the right architects, and people with straight white teeth could organize it all.

The vast selection of fabulous food only confirmed the system in the USA had worked, as there was plenty for everyone, enough to give away, and plenty spare.

It was like living on a film set for a propaganda film and no one ever said, "cut."

Waxed apples, flaunting their pale-green skins like thick Rolls Royce paint, lay next to bunches of radishes flushed with embarrassed. I ignored the perky carrots - all the same color and length – the wispy bundles of dill, soft and feathery-like seaweed and the light, springy parsley waiting for fish.

The stock was never depleted or disheveled, and the odd tub of blueberries or a banana would drop into my basket.

We never cooked in the kitchen and I fantasied about making dishes that I had no idea on how to really make.

These were ingredients that longed for an experienced cook, and I wanted to be that person, but Tim wanted dinner out every night, and I was terrified of ruining his meal.

I could have jumped into the salad leaves and played boule with the letterbox-red tomatoes, but instead I bought a cauliflower with a creamy-white bumpy pure face and took it home with me and put it in the fridge.

Alone, on a shelf, it beamed back at me for about five weeks before decay spoilt its lovely face, and that's when I realized foods here were irradiated, and they did not know what the long-term effects were.

This was a bizarre, unnatural type of longevity, and I was sad when it died.

All the fizzy drinks in lime green plastic bottles, too big for a normal human to lift, stood next to packets of chips and tacos as large as pillows for homeless people, except there were no homeless people around here.

Buying cleaning products demanded some serious study, as each bottle was completely confident of its own success, and I wanted them all.

I never did get to try out their promises, as Tim had already arranged a nice Spanish lady to come in to clean, what was already spotless house, and who spoke no English but enjoyed studying the messages on the bright plastic bottles.

This was life in the USA, my friend.

Sales Office

"Stay in the car, I want to look at something," said Tim as he pulled into a grand entrance and took a sharp right turn onto a no-through road with a roundabout at the end.

He stopped outside a low temporary building covered with generous tropical plants, stepped out of the car and dashed up a few shallow steps, disappearing inside and leaving the engine running.

I swung my legs across the long deep red leather Cadillac seats and looked out of the windows towards nothing but scrubland.

Eventually two figures, deep in conversation, appeared on the steps, and as I leaned forward I saw a tall young woman of about my age. There were a lot of hand gestures.

I was about to open the car door when he glanced in my direction and feverishly beckoned me over.

"Here, come with me. This is my wife, Mel - Mel is in real estate and is Gary's wife." She was full of vitality and stared at me with curious big brown eyes.

We went inside a large open planned office, in the middle of which a huge scale model of the entire development was mounted, including golf courses.
Around the room drawings, maps, and large photos displayed the stunning architecture of each of the villages.

This was Florida living; buying a plot off plan in a golfing community that offered a house and a lifestyle between three-hundred thousand and five million dollars.
On top of that was an annual property tax (a percentage of the value of the house), owner dues for upkeep, plus a golf membership (at least $60,000 and a tennis membership about $5,000 per year).

There was a hush; a feeling of reverence, and telephones kept ringing by the reception desk, answered by velvety voices asking if they can help them, with a willingness that the Samaritans lacked.

A small waiting area, with pastel wicker chairs, water, toilets, and awards beautifully displayed in a lit cabinet, had a couple of prospective new clients arrive.

I leaned over the architect's model but it was too huge to comprehend. Tiny plastic figures depicted dwellers, rows of little Spanish style houses hugged bends in paper roads, and plastic trees divided up the villages.

All around us were glossy photos of azure blue pools, Columbian emerald-green grass, sunsets, and golfers.

"What do you think?" Tim asked, breaking my reverie.
"I don't know, there's so much to take in," I answered, but was he really asking me *if* we should buy a house, or had he decided to and was asking me *which* one? Or was that just a question that meant nothing much at all?

Mel returned with sheets of papers and brochures, smiling like she had just cracked a code.

Taking us over to the 'holding area', she spread them over a table and started talking floor plans. She turned the plans in all directions, and when one was about to make sense, she pulled another from underneath, placed it on top, and started again.
Tim didn't give any of these much attention, but asked a lot of other questions about a whole host of things.

I sat in silence and watched them both alternately like I was at an invisible tennis game, waiting for an outcome.

"We hope you have found something of interest for us, I don't want to waste your time, or mine, you understand. I don't mean to be difficult, but let's weed out the unsuitable ones and see what possibilities are left," Tim was speaking with his fingertips together in an open prayer formation.

He was being really polite because she was pretty but I don't think she realized that.
"You weren't too specific on what your budget will be, so I will go across the board until you have a feeling for how much

buys what," she replied. It seemed like a perfectly good idea to me, and she had directed her words at both of us, which I thought was very considerate of her.

She was very tall, with a warm golden complexion, and she could have sold property off her looks alone if the wives resisted strangling her first.

I smiled enigmatically, excusing myself and wandering off to find the ladies' room. I paused to read names on awards for the last year's sales person and noticed her name was the top of the list. I knew she would not be sparing any effort to reach that target again this year.

Thirty minutes later, papers, mobile phone, and brochures in hand, we made for her car. Tim and I fought for the back seat; he won and I sat in the front.

Swinging around bends that led to boulevards then tree-lined avenues that opened onto fairways, I looked into the distance towards grand and generous properties that beckoned us closer.

I wanted to see them all- even the ones that weren't for sale. Every marble entrance, every double-etched glass door, every elegant flight of blush stone steps, enclosed Italian courtyards decorated with hand-painted tiles and fountains.
If she wanted enthusiastic clients I was first line, but I wasn't sure about the checkbook belonging to man I was with.

It was not all about the owning; it was about the pure pleasure of looking and learning, and my curiosity was overwhelming, but I had to look calm and collected.

We pulled up outside Vintage Isle and each house looked like a mini palazzo; wrought iron doorways laden with bougainvillea and a three-car garage.

Turning to us, she said, "this house has never been lived in. The guy bought two; he needs to sell one and the price is right. Let's go straight in." I didn't need to be asked twice.
The drive was laid with angled brickwork in a soft blush pink and we entered a portico with a twenty-foot double outdoor set in high walls that lead into a courtyard. A pool and fountain that tumbled down the entire wall of Spanish tiles and it looked like a luxury boutique hotel entrance.

A guesthouse with sliding French doors, a small fridge, and air-conditioning stood next to the entrance gates.
It was adorable and I would have been happy just in there and leave the big house to Tim…most of the time.

"That would be great for the kids," she said helpfully, and I smiled, envisaging me trotting across a courtyard serving them food.

We entered a thirty-foot double-etched glass front door, and facing us was an expanse of perfect cream marble like an ice cream cake. I stood transfixed, as on the far end of the room were huge glass French doors that lead out directly onto a terrace and the actual golf course. It was stunning!

"Em…" was the only thing I could say, and I fell into line and followed the others so they would not see how I stopped and stared.

Each bedroom suite had French doors that led back onto the pool in the enclosed courtyard.
There was no furniture, and just thick mushroom-colored carpet-like virgin moss underfoot.

The white bathrooms looked efficient and medicinal, with oversized chrome taps and showerheads spread wide like fountains.

An open-plan kitchen topped with a million light bulbs casted shadows that made the cabinets look like wall sculpture. She was trying to impress me with the quality of the appliances, which were the biggest I had ever seen, but I was already impressed.

The pièce de résistance was the master bedroom on the opposite side of the house away from all the other bedrooms, facing the pool and courtyard. With double doors, one would have been enticed to run naked at dawn and splash in the pool in full view of all the guests.

It had two walk-in closets, which in Europe would have been described as individual rooms; a master bathroom filled with a small quarry of more cream marble, double sinks, and a shower in which you could invite guests and entertain.

"No bidet? What a shame," I said, trying not to be difficult. I had to say something to stifle the screams of delight I felt inside.

"There's plenty of room to have one put in if you want. Fuck, there's enough room to put in a hundred damn bidets!" Tim said walking off, pushing his hands down deep into his pockets.
"Well, I told you it was some house. Thank you so much. I will be in touch. Bye for now," said our glamorous broker, and she left.

We nodded to the owner on the way out. He was the least interesting detail about the whole place - the type of man who could have committed murder and got away with it, because he was so grey and faceless no one would have remembered him enough to identify him.

Non-descript, grey hair, five foot nine inches, pale grey skin, with watery eyes behind steel-rimmed glasses. He stood off in a far corner like a light fitting, hardly spoke, and obviously loved the shade pale mushroom.

This was the smaller of the two houses and his wife only visited twice a year.

He must have done something to earn his money that required great detail and anonymity. In my mind he was spy, and a good one at that.

We walked back out into the hot afternoon sun and the air clawed at our skin.

"Some house right?" Tim said rocking on his heels, hand still deep in his pockets.

"I want to see more things. I'm not really sure, what do you think?" he asked, looking through me.

I hesitated. I wished I had the power to make a decision there and then because the house was breath taking.

Perhaps he could see himself living in such splendor, but did he want to spend all that money to put me in such paradise?

The motto should have been "live in Florida - you already have one foot in heaven."

But Florida came at a price, financially and emotionally, which forever rose and I was not sure we wanted to pay for it.

The Club House

In the center of hundreds of acres of perfection, the hub of all activity was The Clubhouse.

Seeing so many empty houses that showed no signs of life, a few odd passing cars, a lonely jogger or two prompted one to ask, "where are all the people?"

Pulling up to a huge Spanish-style pink building, heavily laden with a mass of blooming bougainvillea, a smart young valet leapt out to park the car.

Under a huge stone canopy, large terracotta steps led the way through beds of pinks up to impressive twenty-five-foot double wooden doors, which opened into sub-zero temperatures like a wall of invisible ice.

A deafening noise of hundreds of unseen people filled the air, thundering and vibrating.

Elegant ceilings above us were studded with a million spotlights shining like twenty-four-hour stars and flooding the halls with light. A huge marble table with a four-foot flower arrangement obscured the view, but the noise kept coming.

We entered a pale green, soft pink dining room, with thirty-five-foot high glass windows showing a view of the golf course and right across the greens.

Fifty-five-foot buffet tables displayed every dish known to man, laden with cruise ship-sized platters filled to capacity.

Waves of eager excited chatter washed towards us and across the room. Food obviously excited people, as large portions called for strong voices.

Baskets of breads were hurried to waiting tables to replace others as soon as the wicker showed.

Joints of meats carved from small dinosaurs fed carnivorous dinners holding up plates that consumed fields of salads.

Young men and women ran like emergency staff in between tables in case a patient passed out from malnutrition.

"Hey miss!"
"Hey there fella!"

Rang out the chorus from each table, indisposed with feverish chatter.

I was shivering with cold, but I had not noticed, being so flabbergasted at the sight before me.

Moving on to explore more, I wandered down wide corridors of pink walls and moss green carpets. They led surreptitiously in different directions, with small graceful engraved signs on plaques, promising pleasures.
Card room, Spa, Gym, Therapy room, Library…each one I wanted or needed, so I headed for the gym.

High arched windows with wood surrounds looked out onto a tropical rain forest of twisted foliage, thick and alive. Through the branches I could see a lake-sized azure swimming blue pool lying placid and undisturbed.

Lines of obedient treadmills were in front of the windows, each one responsible for hundreds of miles of travel, and yet they had not moved an inch.
They seemed to be arranged in pecking order - the best ones getting the front row views, and cleverly the tinted window glass was one-way, so the pool bathers could not see in and make out the figures exercising inside through the tangles vines. I am sure one group would have made the other feel guilty for one reason or another.

The machines stood silent and motionless; the room looked new and unused.

Neat rows of weights lined one wall, and charts above gave instructions on what to do with them in drawings showing muscle groups in various colors.

I thought a pin-up calendar of thin girls might have motivated us more.

This room obviously did not want to be disturbed, so I left and followed another green corridor, but I ran out of time and turned back.

Unknown to me, this room was going to be my refuge and I would be in here and not just to exercise.

Croissant for Kay

Jumping up at the sound of the alarm at 7am was no hardship when a clear blue sky dotted with puffballs clouds was your welcome.

By 8.15 a.m. a line of Mercedes', BMWs, Lexus' and other luxury cars were scrambling for spots on the car park closet to the courts.

There were plenty of 'hellos' being exchanged, with many familiar faces that, as yet, had no names.

A crowd had gathered by the noticeboard with a lot of questions without any answers being exchanged outside the tennis shop.

"What is this?" I asked Tim.

"A Round Robin, and you are in it," he said, and disappeared to interrogate other people.

The head pro came out to take questions and could only cope with the front row.

"Saturday at 11am, mixed men's and ladies' doubles. Sign up if you haven't already!" He shouted.

My heart missed a beat and I felt a chill sweep up my neck.

Tim had signed us both up for this and I knew this would be my moment of utter public shame.

My mind raced as to what illness I could invent, what symptoms I needed to have, what limb I could blame, so I could become a spectator.

I would have to check myself into a clinic for a few days and actually get wired up, as he would have me play in a plaster cast.

Walking to Friday's tennis clinic in a trance I was waiting for a brainwave. Saturday was tomorrow.

I asked all the girls in the clinic if they had also signed up, and they said 'yes' they had.

A very tall, thin, quaky woman in her forties whom had previously been friendly was my target. She had very thin flesh covering a strangely shaped skeleton and needed a bit more fat to cover it up. She was a bit confused about nothing in particular, and gave the impression of being a few seconds behind everything happening around her.

"Are you joining this thing on Saturday?" I asked disdainfully.

"What thing?" Only she could not understand the question.

"The round robin, square pigeon, long sparrow, whatever they call it," I replied.

"Oh that…. you're funny. I don't know, as my daughter has a party. She needs a dress, so I should get her fitted." I walked away, as this story could go on until Saturday and I only wanted a 'yes' or 'no,' so I approached short, darker, athletic women who seemed to talk to everyone.

"Oh sure it will be fun, someone has to lose and it may as well be us!" I liked her immediately, and no more than five foot four in height she radiated all the energy in the world.

"You're from England aren't you? I will be spending the summer in France, studying French. My boyfriend has a place in Monaco where his parents live. Do you speak French?

Perhaps we can meet and all play tennis there?" She asked.

"Yes, we go to the south of France around June. My French is adequate, but my tennis is pretty poor," I answered, my mind tingling at the thought of being asked to play tennis in France. I, the worst player in the club, had an invitation for tennis!

Only the Americans could extend such impractical invitations, from two bad players with three words of French between them, for the Cote d'Azur in the summer without even knowing each other's surnames.

The blood pumped through my veins and I fingered the strings on my racquet, to give the air of a real player.

"So I will see you Saturday, and maybe we can be partners. My name is Kay," she said, smiling.

It was my turn to be friendlier and I asked her why the tall thin lady seemed so confused.

"That's because Randy's husband has just walked out on her, giving her a two million dollar house fully paid for, and she doesn't know what day of the week it is," her eyes twinkled and her teeth gleamed with the glee and knowledge of such privileged information.

Glancing back at the tall, gawky, woman whose bones stuck out in all directions, she was still completely self-absorbed.

I didn't need her to help through the Round Robin, as mentally, I was already playing in Monaco.

Funny how even the useless can emotionally move on quickly...

Diet coke for Eric & Sonia

One late afternoon hot and sticky after playing, or pretending to play in my case, we all raced for the last empty table and grabbed the chairs like they were life rafts.

"What y'all be a'vin?" Asked our ample waitress in a low drawl.
"Diet coke!"
"Diet coke!"
"Diet coke!"
"Soda!"

Called out each person one by one. It was a rainbow of one fizzy drink after another.

"Water for me please, no ice," I said, to change the flow.
"What's that!?" She looked to the others at the table to provide
a reliable translation. I always got the same reaction, so I
repeated my order, very slowly.

While I was here I might as well re-hydrate, detox, and
cleanse all in one go. I would get the 'tucks', but I wouldn't rot
in Coke in the meantime.

"It's a tennis BBQ tonight at six, so who's going?" Tim threw
out the question to the table and there was a show of hands,
except for Eric's.
"You're not coming? Why not? You've *got* to come tonight -
make an effort!" Tim exclaimed, straight from the heart.
"I'll ask my wife, Sonia, but I know she hates these things and
she doesn't like to be around the tennis crowd. I doubt it," he
looked down at the table and stopped talking. He had missed
every event, and we were beginning to feel sorry for him.

He was the first to arrive at the courts every morning at 8am
and the last to leave; his playing was improving dramatically,
despite injuring himself from over playing.

I wondered if his wife was s dragon or something, as he was
reasonable-looking and left alone all the time, which could be
dangerous as this was Florida and full of desperate women.

"I have to go home to change into a dress, it's really late," I
said to Tim as I moved my things to go.
"Don't be ridiculous!" Came the reply, and in no uncertain
terms, I knew that was end of that. "You will go in tennis
clothes like everyone else; just put on a clean set. No one gets
dressed up for these things."

I could never imagine going to an event in the UK sports
clothes, but this was the USA and the formal rules of Europe
were left behind.

Sure enough at six, all the players arrived looking exactly as they had done that morning in more tennis outfits. This was the season's tennis BBQ, and I would have looked ludicrous in high heels, satin, and pearls....I had to learn and learn quickly.

My world, and my people were not here, and I had to adjust, fit in, understand the protocol then smile, listen, and keep smiling.

So I did.

❀   ❀   ❀

When seeing reports on CNN on families living in war-torn countries, houses blown apart and reduced to rubble, I think some Americans actually believe they aren't real pictures, but more of an 'overseas thing' shown to make them feel guilty.

The members of a country club raise arms if the pool cuts back on towels, if the tennis times are reduced by unnecessary building works, or god forbid if there was bad weather.

Let them paint at night, let them dig in silence, or let them clean after midnight, but interruptions were not accepted without a lot of protests. I happened to agree, because this level of organizing was 'art', not just a matter of being efficient.

It could be seen in the major casinos in Vegas, Disney World, great shopping Malls, NYC skyscrapers, hotel chains, and in golf clubs in Florida.

After an unexpected afternoon shower, the sun filtered back through the clouds and the water melted away into ripples of gold, slipping into cracks and out of sight.

A single white egret screeched high into the cleansed air, preened itself and stared at nothing.

With no seasonal changes, people mysteriously got thinner and younger.

The only way to mark time was by noting who started on what team with what handicap, and with what car that season.

This was Florida living, in a golfing community, behind a security wall, and I was beginning to lose my nationality.

❆ ❆ ❆

Pulling up to a free standing 1950s diner in a parking lot, I was hardly overjoyed but too hungry to complain.

"Names!" shouted the middle-aged seasoned waitress with sun-damaged wrinkled skin and an ironed apron at the door. "How many?" She didn't bother to look up from her clipboard; she didn't need to, she could feel us all. "No tables for two for forty-five minutes, only a table for four in five minutes. Who's next?"

Tim looked at the couple behind us, asked them if they would share a table, and screamed "Four! We are four! We just grew two more!"

That was it. We were in, seated, holding menus, and we discussed the food.

"We come here all the time. You will love this. You like Nova, bagels and cream cheese?" The man and woman gushed at us.

His eyes were beaming and glistening with the excitement from what was to come.

He ordered for the table and Tim readily agreed because the man ordered more than we would have, and it saved Tim finding his glasses.

"Fresh juice, coffee, scrambled eggs, poppy bagels, fresh onions, Nova Scotia salmon - all to come out at the same time." He yelled and it was music to my ears.

"Coming right up," said our waitress and we all watched her leave and go straight to the kitchen, put in the order and return with the coffees.

As the food arrived I picked up one plate and began to share it with a fork delicately.
Tim poured the entire portion on my plate, threw a bagel on top and said "Eat! That's not to share that's *one portion*"

I laughed nervously and I saw a shadow of deep pity cross their eyes.

"Poor child she has never had a whole plate of salmon to herself-it must be the rationing in Europe after the war" they were thinking.

I immediately fell in love with the 1950's dinner and swore to come here at least once a week if not more.

We all fell silent and I learnt a new meaning of 'heaven.' This is what I will dream about during future tennis games.

"You both play tennis?" The man beamed his question at us from a cherub-like face, with little hair left.
"Yes," we both answered at the same time.

He was essentially a large ball, mostly stomach on sturdy legs and in his late sixties.
"Good, we will play one day. How about tomorrow? Do we have a game for tomorrow?" He quickly turned to his wife who smiled sweetly, like a 14-year-old girl trapped in a sixty-something body.

She was embarrassed by his forthright attitude, but it was his attitude in life that got her living in a golf resort behind a wall.

"No, I don't think so," she replied sheepishly.
"Good. By the way, I am Joe and this is my wife, Cora," he held out his hand for Tim to shake.
"Pleased to meet you, I'm sure," Cora added, having been forced her entire life to meet total strangers.

We introduced ourselves and we were pleased to be invited to play, even against such a mature couple. I was more than a generation younger and perhaps even appeared to be a reasonable player. I felt guilty for deceiving them, so I mumbled that I had not been playing long.

"Nonsense, she's fabulous. With that figure she's a devil on the tennis court. Don't believe a word!" Tim proclaimed, and he put his arm around me like a vice to discourage any contradictions on my part.

I was doomed, again.

He was American and I came from planet Mars and everyone was laughing.

Four sets of gleaming white ivories caught the sunlight in false smiles, topped with moistened eyes watching their new opponents every move to assess strengths and weaknesses.

As we left Joe said;

"Until tomorrow. I will get the court, leave it all to me. Won't we darling? Come along then."

His sturdy brown legs carried his rounded belly off, with that cherub face and beady-brown eyes.

Cora was rounded, but carried her fat like a burden; her large brown eyes were dull, as she did not look forward to the 8.30am game tomorrow as her husband was.

"What did you tell them that for? Are you completely mad?" I bluntly demanded to his profile.

"Don't be ridiculous, you'll be fine. Just hit the ball back over the net and leave the rest to me." He was literally going to have to play singles against a doubles pair.
"It's the net that's in my way!" I pleaded.

I was resigned, but sick to the stomach after all that great food, for being so hopelessly mismatched.

Another struggle set in paradise, and I thought of changing my name to 'Ridiculous.'

Cool Pools for Claudine and Prince Albert

The two main pool areas, located next to each other, were tucked away privately behind the clubhouse in lush gardens, mature tropical plants, and fully-grown palm trees.

The larger pool was for children, young family groups, and a baby shallow pool, with a small gate, which no one ever seemed to use.

The 'adults only' pool was slightly smaller, heavily protected with greenery, and hardly anyone swam in it.

The ten-seater Jacuzzi was always full and therefore very unappealing to me.
We positioned ourselves far away from everyone, right in the middle of them both.

I avoided small children in water, as you often ended up a volunteer lifeguard for selfish parents who never noticed you plunged into freezing water to save a kid who had been previously annoying you all day.

At the pool's edge mothers with no makeup and hair pulled into bands with protruding bellies rummaged through bags full of domestic nonsense while father lay motionless, baking in the hot sun until a shapely pair of legs walked by.

At the other end were the older retired folks, in Boca for the season as 'snow birds' escaping the perilous winters in the North.

It was a frightening sight and a sign of what we would become.

In Europe older folks seemed to keep their clothes on even if they were deeply tanned and looked more outdoors and healthy.

We had a huge tree for shade, plenty of towels and water, a few bottles of lotion, and we were settled for the afternoon; it was heaven.

Noises faded into the background, merging together like oil paints, with an odd shriek or scream piercing the air like a distant parrot in branches high above us.
As a soft breeze tiptoed all over us, just enough to fan the hot spots, and the tensions seeped out of my extremities.

Forty minutes later and regaining consciousness, I heard a voice that went through my skull right into my brain, so I turned my bloated body and opened one eye.

To my horror, all that empty space had now been filled with chairs, tables, and a group of about eight men and women in their early fifties. They were from New Jersey, and all uncomfortably close to me.

"Hello," said a man next to me, hardly turning his head.

"Hello," I replied, leaning on my elbows and staring at the pool.

They were obviously old friends but I still hadn't identified that shrill voice.

From behind big Versace glasses I peered around and there she was. A head of rich auburn hair, flashing white teeth, very thick burgundy lipstick, and small, round black tinted spectacles, so her eyes were not visible.

She was watching, not being watched, except by me.

Some of the men just languished, fighting off an afternoon's sleep in the baking sun, and most of the women had formed an inner circle, furnishing each other with the juicy gossip missed out from last year's reunion.

"No, that was his third wife, not his second."

"Are you sure? She told me differently."

"Yes, because the two daughters were from the first wife who died."

"She died!? I thought she lived here in Florida?"

"She did. Then she died. Anyway, I saw him playing golf *and* he's going chapter eleven."

And so these fantastic tales went on, each more tragic than the last. I was becoming part of the audience and wanted to ask my own questions.

"Didn't she serve him with divorce papers?"

"How did his children not know?"

"Is it legal to marry twice?"

"How long can you live with that kind of serious illness?"

It never stopped. They covered every experience known to man, and lawyers, and it was fascinating.

The entire time the auburn head bobbed up and down and I notice she was a petite woman with the energy of a tiger.

She played the crowd, only speaking to those with something interesting to contribute, let the boring ones listen and seem to know more that the rest of them put together.

She sat nearest to the women and it was impossible to say which man was her husband.

The laughter died down as the heat sapped the energy from the most resilient. Some people wandered off for drinks, some looked for shade, and one or two just slept.

"Where's Michael?" Asked a blonde woman with no make-up and large green eyes. She leaned forward, looking into the distance.

"He was here a minute ago. I just saw him," someone answered from behind.

She held on to her bone-thin brown ankles at the end of runner's legs. She did not have an ounce of flesh on her bones, just thin hanging skin, and her eyes were sad like a puppy's, not desperate enough to get up and find Michael, but still counting the time that passed.

Who knew why she searched for him? But I thought it was very sweet.

The auburn hair was quieter, deep in conversation; with her hand on the knee of a woman she was telling a story while delicately holding her captive.

With white flesh against thick black hair and huge almond eyes, she looked like Cleopatra of Egypt, and was listening intently, enjoying every word.

Some women don't know they are beautiful, or are too modest to admit it, and she was such a creature now in her fifties, plump and with a body that didn't look that often into a mirror.

As I was studying all this, a rogue New York Times paper cartwheeled over the patio and stopped it self by clinging to my legs like an octopus.

The more I struggled to break free, the closer it clung, until sheet by sheet, it had to be peeled off.

"Are you okay? Oh my god, honey your paper's blown away," one woman called out.

Two leaned over to see better and a man came over to rescue me, or save the paper, I was not sure which.

"No, no, I'm fine. Thank you, don't get up."

"Are you British?" The man asked.

"Yes, I am."

"Oh how lovely. Here, let me help you get rid of that. Are you visiting?"

"No I live part of the time in the US."

"Oh how lovely," he said again. He and the auburn woman looked at each other.

"What 'part of the time' is that exactly?" The auburn lady, with the small dark glasses and the very big expensive smile, asked. "My name is Claudine, and that is my husband, Albert," she said, waving over to grey, ordinary man asleep and uninterested.

I didn't realize it at the time, but I had just secured my place in their next year's reunion stories and that clinging newspaper would alter the course of our winter.

❄   ❄   ❄

House questions

"Have you bought your house yet?" Boomed a voice so loud it nearly shattered the glass tabletop I was sitting at.

I slowly looked up to a fat, ugly, sweaty figure that had just finished a game. It was Paul, who by sure twist of fate had spent years in the insurance business, sold everything, and retired early in the Florida sunshine from New Jersey.

His most glamorous possession was a convertible black
Mercedes sport, which was a gorgeous new car, and showed a
degree of taste for a man who had none.
I think he loved it more than his wife, as I recalled that she
had never been seen sitting in it.

He had asked the multimillion-dollar question, and I felt ten
pairs of eyes leave their bagels and cream cheese and look
over my way.

Demanding an answer to a question before opening up a
conversation, without the usual niceties, was something I was
quite used to by now.

He wiped his gorilla-shaped neck with a towel and his
overgrown, childlike form was ugly and instructive.

"Which house? There are so many," I threw the questions
straight back.

"Well, I guess you haven't made up your mind yet. I heard
you were looking." He boomed back at me.

"We certainly are," I smiled enigmatically to conclude the
conversation. I turned away and waved to no one in particular
in the distance behind him.

"Bye Paul," I said. I didn't see him leave.

The fact was I had no more idea than they did. In private we
never talked together about buying a house - it was almost like
the topic was taboo, and the odd time I brought it up he got
busy or walked away.

We were looking at least three days a week, but never with
appointments, just impromptu drop-ins to sales offices dotted

around the area. I went along because I loved looking at the houses, and liked that the sales assistants were trying to work out if he was actually a client or not-an question I was also asking myself.

❈   ❈   ❈

Christmas was coming up and I had to leave for Europe to see the family. Tim wanted to stay in Florida to play tennis and see his family who were visiting from Washington.

We had now settled into the rental house, but never spent any more time there other than to sleep, shower, and change clothes; and certainly never to eat.

The pool lay undisturbed, save for one leaf that had fallen through the screen and floated aimlessly onto the pale blue surface. I promised myself to swim every week, but as time went by, the idea of climbing into a huge pool of freezing water began to horrify me as much as it had done Tim.

The screen doors remained shut, but I did open the bedroom French doors a couple of times when he was in the shower. I always felt I was inviting a huge fight, so I always went back and closed them.

I never had a lot of time to see the galaxy of stars every night through the bathroom skylight as I was becoming exhausted from the daily and nightly pace. For some reason, people seemed to rush from activity to activity so as not to miss anything.

I suppose Paul chose to ask me the question, as he knew he was not going to get any answers from Tim.

None of us were.

Shrimp with Louis and Katarina

"You haven't looked at the ocean? He hasn't shown you the beachfront apartments? Oh boy, some people wouldn't live in a country club if you gave it to them free! It's a whole different thing. Isn't it? It's a whole different thing. Not for us honey?"

Asked Louis to his wife, gravely concerned Tim and I were making the biggest mistake of our lives.

"No, of course we wouldn't live on the ocean," Kat answered. "Who heard of such an idea? Where would you go for golf and tennis every day? How could *we* live on the ocean?" she replied like he had asked her to dig up her grandmother and breathe life back into her corpse.

"Well, you join a club for one thing.
What's wrong with joining a good club that has great golf and tennis?" Tim provided both the answer and then posed another question.

"There are plenty of great clubs nearby Kat. You don't know what you're talking about - there's that great one the Silverman's joined that costs a bloody fortune, and the miserable bastard doesn't invite me to play golf there anymore." Louis laughed.

"You'd pay $80,000 to join his club? You told me the place stinks and they have no idea how to run a proper club, but just laze around and drink Martinis," said Kat.

She dismissed the fabulous beachside golf club, who with a few Martini drinkers who all sounded like they had their priorities just right to me.

"No, I didn't say that, I said…"

"Forget what you said, the fact is there are plenty of great clubs around all begging for new members. That's the least of my worries. The question is do you want to *drive* to the club? That's the point." Tim laid down another question, so difficult that for a moment there was a brief silence.

"What's wrong with driving?" I just had to ask.
They all looked at me with horror, as if I had exploded, and then instantly forgave the question because I was *foreigner* and really didn't know.

"You don't *want* to drive," she whispered like I had committed a huge faux pas. "Not to a club."

"You see, the point of being in Florida is that you fall out of bed and get to the courts early before it gets hot. Now, you can't make an 8am game if you damn well have to have to start driving down the I95 to get to tennis!" Tim banged the table, and the waiter ran over.

"It's not *that* far. You're not going *all* the way down the 95. Who plays at 8am? It doesn't get warm until February and you can play until 10am." Louis told him.

"Bull! I never play after half past eight, it gets hot by ten, and that's when you finish," explained Kat.

"You're both full of crap. The fact is you have to park then check in for a court. By the time you get some balls, it's a whole bloody mess!" Tim declared.

I watched, I listened, I learned, but I wanted to see for myself.

Driving to a tennis club in a convertible Mercedes under blue skies, in a club that served Martinis didn't put my blood pressure up too much, but that was going to be saved for other things I had not yet noticed in paradise.

The Happiest Hour

One Friday night at the Clubhouse party we backed off towards the middle of the room, holding onto our drinks and watching a clamor of people that had formed a human wall at one end of the salon.

Had someone passed out? Was the crowd helping? We ambled over to the far end and peered around to see a hundred arms reaching and grabbing, twisting like an octopus in a desperate struggle.

What could cause such panic amongst mature, rich, well dressed inhabitants of a luxury development such as this?

Of course - it was the free finger food buffet.

A very tall young black boy dressed in crisp whites called to the crowd to make way.

He was carrying a big deep silver tray of mini pizzas, which he unloaded onto the table, only just making it out alive as they closed in after him like a voracious tide of starved rats.

A few people staggered away holding plates piled high, with enough to feed a small African village, and made their way to tables of waiting friends who leaned in, examined the offerings and selected morsels with lighting speed.

I made my way along the line, passing great bowls where the odd carrot stick lay lifeless, streaks of pink dip lay between beaten crushed lettuce leaves and the odd corpse of a squashed mushroom, left bleeding.

Huge empty platters were graveyards to a few silver dollies, sad bridesmaids discarded after the wedding feast.

Slithers of salmon scattered the white table cloth in a bid to escape, bundles of parsley became rolling tumble weed, looking for a corner to settle in - it was a pitiful sight.

Salvaging what we could, we shuffled towards crowded tables and spotted one spare chair, which Tim grabbed and forced me into.

The room was buzzing with members greeting each other like lost relations, while others sat staring, watching them and guarding their stash of hors d'oeuvres like gold.

It was like being in a war before the bombs had been dropped. It was pure panic, pure survival, and pure animal instinct - in luxury.

"Why are we here?" I asked Tim, who just shrugged his shoulders.

"To meet people," he eventually replied.

Being with me made him see how absurd the whole thing was, and I felt sorry for him, as I bet up until now he had really enjoyed all those happy Fridays, and done very well at the hors d'oeuvres table, as he was a fighter…I had ruined all for him.

Seeing More Houses with Claudine and Albert

"What do you think?" I asked Claudine, as by now her and Albert were so keen on us buying a house, they came along to the viewings with us. I presumed they were bored and, like me, enjoyed people spending money and looking at houses.

"Oh my God, Corian! CO-RI-AN!"
Claudine shouted up to the thirty-five-foot high ceiling.

It was the kitchen counter top, which looked pretty ordinary to me and nothing like a good marble or enduring granite. They explained why I should be so excited, and I was not.

"This is the greatest shower. There is enough room for a shower party!"

Albert giggled and went off to see another wing of the house.

"So you like this?" Tim asked with his hands on his hips. Was he offering it to me, or just asking my opinion?

"Do you?" I replied, but I really meant, "Are you ever going to buy a house?
Everyone, including me, would love to know."

"That's not what I asked. Come on, let's talk seriously, what do you think?"

"I think it's the most beautiful house I have ever seen," I said quietly, like I was confessing to a sin.

"Do you really? I 'm not sure I like being on the golf course like this. All those balls could be dangerous you know?" he said looking at a carpet of thick, undulating green grass with not a golfer in sight.

Claudine walked back across the cream marble silently in her white canvas sneakers. He asked the same question in her direction.
"*What*! Are you *insane*? Come here! Do you think you will ever see a golf ball? No! Show me the golf balls! Do you see any golf balls? Broken windows or what?" She waved her hands toward the perfect scene that looked like a hand-woven carpet, without rabbit foot prints, least of all golf balls.

"I can't even see any golfers," said Albert in a dry tone, and smiled at me.

"Well, *you* couldn't if they hit you in the face!" She snapped back at him and he shuffled off, happy with his remark.

My attention returned to the person presently running my life, by absurdly looking for the one killer golf ball.

He looked at me for support and I didn't give him any. This was a very expensive house, and who knew the parameters of his budget.

They all thought that I knew but I didn't, but still they kept peppering me with questions.

In my mind, this house was so beautiful that only money could be a reasonable obstacle...not golf balls.

Ocean Views

I had always felt an incredible peace in Florida's climate, which made me feel at home.

I was that last dinosaur who waded through the Everglades just before the meteor hit, and now when the huge Jurassic ocean-crossing birds flew overhead, I would look skyward in admiration, even during tennis.

The constant blue skies, punctuated with white puffballs, had my attention, so I spent more time looking up than down, which suited me, as it helped me to avoid people.

Maybe like all Brits, I had spent too much of my life under a thick blanket of grey and was desperate to get into the light, the Italianate rays, sunsets, and a dawn worth jumping out of bed for.

The Atlantic Ocean never appealed to me as I found it threatening, not even an environment for animals as even the waves crashing on the beach sounded like warnings and frightened me to death.

Cruise ships continually passed on the far-off horizon and shone in the sun like jewels, but I wished them well and had absolutely no interest in joining them.

They never looked that big.

Miami Beach apartment blocks are huge long rectangular boxes, sub-divided into thousands of smaller boxes, facing the ocean at the front and the fascinating Inter-coastal waterway facing west. They often looked like luxury prisons, but I resisted saying so.

The new generations of condos are super luxurious, super smart, super expensive, and offer something to everyone.

South Beach, full of 1930s deco architecture, was saved from being demolished by a shear miracle after Gianni Versace bought and rented a spectacular building on the front and made it his own. South Beach never looked back, and from then on, we all missed the boat and wished we had bought something, but the truth was we didn't have the guts; the area could have gone both ways.

We drove up and down the coast, looking again at ocean-side buildings, which I found fascinating because there were so many and the overall investment alone was staggering.

It was like a machine. They pulled down buildings in the US, that we in the UK would have given a lick of paint to and resold expensively and expected the client to be grateful.

The Real Estate agents all pointed out the view like we were blind and had not noticed the five or six trillion gallons of salty water right outside the door.
"You know, there's nothing to see once the sun goes down," said Tim defiantly.
He was right. Oceans go black at night, and all the really pretty lights are on the East side along the Inter-coastal that is cheaper.

The agent didn't answer him, and I thought, *"well, there's a client who's not buying today"*.

The Last Village

"So what *are* you going to do?" the senior manager Harry said. The real estate office was beginning to warm up with three bodies defying the air conditioning.

I gazed around and looked at all the awards, neatly framed in teak diploma-sized frames arranged in rows along the walls.

"I must get some of those, they look really good in an office or library, because no one actually reads the print, they just look for a stamp and big signature", I thought to myself.

He also had some very nice engraved plates declaring him Sales Person of the Year, but now he was really earning his money.

Gone was the pretty blonde who had helped us in the beginning; we have barely seen even a glimpse of her these days. She had handed us over to her boss and I didn't blame her; it showed excellent judgment.

Tim had deposited five different checks on five different houses simultaneously, all being held on deposit for seven days each, and all the checks were returnable.

I wanted all five houses, starting with the most expensive one. By now every person in the club had shown us their houses, introduced their neighbors, given us details on what extras they had negotiated with the builder and told us the best price to pay.

I smiled to give encouragement when the conversation went from money back to kitchen worktops again.

"I told you, this *is* the best surface they do. Marble will cost you more and give you the same look," Harry's hairspray was going limp, the room heated up again, and he deeply wished he now sold anything other than real estate.

Looking for the ladies' room, I got up and wandered over to the architect's scale model in the center of the sales office.

Another new couple walked in and was guided over to the model with its impressive layout of houses and gorgeous golf course.

As they were left for a few minutes to look at it, dreams took over their heads, dreams that bonded them, and dreams that separated them.

She compared houses from left to right, judging the neighbors, then passed by the one million dollar villages, and went over to the cheaper ones.

He lingered at the golf course, and inspected and traced his route along wavy little paths in his imaginary golf cart back onto the fairway.

He probably booked an early tee-off time, and didn't rush home too soon, while she met up with the girls to get her nails painted again.

They met again around the other side of the table and simultaneously noticed me, no doubt trying to place me in a particular village with young children and bicycles.

A mental note flushed across their eyes; avoid villages with young children, as this was their dream retirement home and a promised heaven.

I went back inside the sales office where blue prints were everywhere, and they were now looking at empty plots of land.

"This is the last house, and it's reasonably priced for a quick sale so we can move onto our next project a couple of miles away," Harry was holding in there and I admired his tenacity.

"So, why can't we look at that?" Tim did not want to move into a new project, as he knew it would be a building site for three years or more.

"We've not broken ground, and believe me, it's not you're thing," the manager replied and I agreed as I couldn't take anymore.

"Okay, show me so I can be certain," Tim had a way of keeping people on a path they wanted to jump from. He understood the power of a financial incentive and must have sold carrots to donkey merchants in a past life. I just wanted to see if anyone actually got to nibble on his carrots.

Harry had all those lovely plates and certificates, and he was going the extra mile and I admired him for it, so I tried to take his mind off the fact it was late Friday afternoon, the traffic was bad, and his wife had called a couple of times.

We drove up to the Northern gate and I thought after traipsing every inch of this club I was able to do sales myself.

Stopping at three show houses facing west the newly planted gardens looked like transplant victims waiting to heal.

Harry struggled with several sets of keys and we went inside.

Straight through the house windows at the far end opened onto gleaming lime-green grass in the last of the sun's rays. Green was for go, and it beckoned me forward.

The end wall was all glass, and I stood at the fence doors looking out as a flame-red ball of a molten gold sun dropped reluctantly over the horizon.

It was if it had been waiting for us, or me at least.
I could hear men's footsteps in other rooms figuring out which bedroom was which, and where the dressing rooms and bathrooms would be.

The patio had hexagonal tiles around a long pool only thirty feet from the kitchen doors.

Just after the pool were railings onto the golf course and a small lake that looked no more than three feet deep. It was perfectly still with a pure white, tall, willowy egret preening itself at the water's edge.

In the sunset, simplicity and tranquility had a stillness twinned with silence.

The black reflection of distant trees shone on the water, and the whole area was devoid of life, save the colonial egret and I.

PART 2

OUT NOW

$0.99

http://www.amazon.com/BEHIND-WALL-PART-Dame-DJ-ebook/dp/B01DECTWMC/ref=sr_1_1?s=books&ie=UTF8&qid=1459312408&sr=1-1&keywords=behind+the+wall+part+2

About the Author

Dame DJ

Please join us at

www. DJBooks.Club

sign up for a free eBook

Contact;

damedj@DJBooks.club

Dame DJ describes herself as "married young, divorced young, had two children young, starved young, remarried a couple more times, & lived in different countries to learn about life"

Book *'Downsize to Freedom'* FREE eBook Part 1 (Part 2) was written after she liquidated, removed all financial obligations, sold what she thought to be overpriced assets and "downsized" - to everyone's horror.

Gourmands on the Run! FREE Part 1 (Part 2 out now) Is about a journey through France, from Paris to Monaco by car, visiting the best hotels & restaurants and illustrated with her original watercolors.

AUDIO book to be released 20ᵗʰ April read by the lovely Sharon Hoyland.

'To be, or not to be Single. That is my Question?' FREE Part 1 (Part 2) eBook is about going in, and coming out of relationships, with some damage control.

AUDIO book out now read by the great voice of John Bico.

'Percy the Pea and Other Friends' FREE eBook is a children's eBook about healthy eating and illustrated with her own watercolor paintings.

AUDIO book now out beautifully read by Dorothy to keep those kids eating!

'Behind the Wall' Parts 1 & 2 & 3 is a factual eBook story describing the truth and revelations about moving into a Florida gated golf community.

'The Dope Diet' new **FREE Part 1 (Part 2 out now) Ebook**
The 'The Dope Diet' is an intimate diary of a young English man David Grey and his struggles with smoking dope.
Tragically he lost more than 8 kilos, money, family, friends and nearly his sanity during his journey, crusade for legalization and acceptance.

Our guest author is

DAVID GREY

New book

THE POT HOLE.

A Pot Delusion.

David Grey gives us a very personal and revealing account of his two year drug habit in The Pot Hole as he describes his marijuana use, its potential addictiveness and consequences many pot smokers are likely to suffer. David's honest insight into his conflict of wanting to advocate the legality and end prohibition of marijuana whilst struggling with the personal conflicts brought on by the dependence on a destructive drug habit. The Pot Hole gives us a fascinating intimate glimpse into the mind of a pot user and illustrates the conflicting perspectives of addiction and the powerful seduction of this forbidden plant. Following him for two years from his initial introduction by his pretty girlfriend CC in romantic Barcelona to isolation in a French mountain village we journey with him along a bumpy route all too familiar with drug issues.

http://www.amazon.com/Pot-Hole-Dope-Delusion-ebook/dp/B01CH93S8C/ref=sr_1_1?s=books&ie=UTF8&qid=1458412219&sr=1-1&keywords=the+pot+hole

----

Individual support & confidential discussions can be arranged details on

www.DJBooks.Club

7 days advance booking needed on GMT
$65 per hour non-members
$50 for members
$40 the 1st day of every month

request dates via;

damedj@DJBooks.Club

**Your reviews are important
please leave your kind words at
<u>Amazon review page.</u>**

<u>Join us on Twitter</u>

@PercyThePea
@GourmandsOnRun
@NotToBeSingle
@DownsizeToFree
@_Behind_TheWall
@thedopediet
@davidgrey999

Printed in Great Britain
by Amazon